W9-AVL-928

How to Hug

By
Maryann Macdonald

Illustrated by
Jana Christy

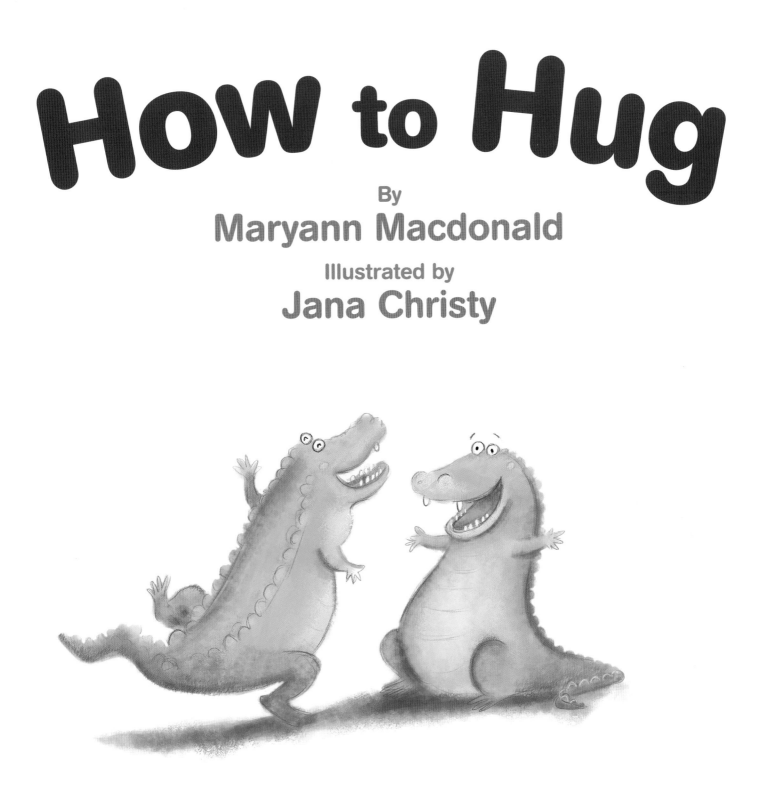

Marshall Cavendish Children

Marshall Cavendish Corporation
99 White Plains Road, Tarrytown, NY 10591
www.marshallcavendish.us/kids

Library of Congress Cataloging-in-Publication Data
Macdonald, Maryann.
How to hug / by Maryann Macdonald;
illustrated by Jana Christy. — 1st ed.
p. cm.
Summary: The reader is invited to consider some
things about when, who, and how to hug and also
advised to be prepared to receive one in return.
ISBN 978-0-7614-5804-3
[1. Hugging—Fiction.] I. Christy, Jana, ill. II. Title.
PZ7.M1486Ho 2011   [E]—dc22   2010016135

The illustrations are rendered digitally.

Book design by Vera Soki
Editor: Margery Cuyler

Printed in China (E)
First edition
1 3 5 6 4 2

Marshall Cavendish
Children

For the huggers in my life . . .
you know who you are
—M.M.

For John, Harry, and Hugo,
whom I like to hug best
—J.C.

When you're happy or sad,
hugs can show how you feel, but . . .

hugs can be tricky!
Never hug anyone too tight . . .

and don't get stuck either.

Try not to freeze up and don't . . .

hold on too long.
Learn how to let go.

Never hug anyone who's angry.
It can take time to get over it,

so just be patient.

Some creatures are too shy for hugging . . .

or too prickly.

Never try to hug too many people at once.

Some may only want a hand to hold . . .

or a kiss on the cheek.

If you don't want a hug, it's okay to say no . . .

but if you do give a hug,
you will usually get one back.

You might get a kiss, too.

So be ready!

Some special hugs are bear hugs,

guess-who hugs,

sideways hugs,

sandwich hugs,

and leg hugs.

Hugs can be hard as a rock . . .

or soft as a pillow.

Dogs like hugs.

Most cats don't.

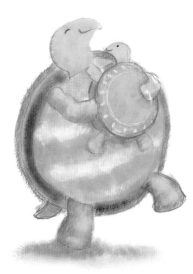

Babies are born
to be hugged.

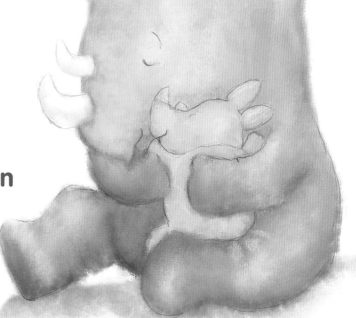

**When it's time for a hug,
open your heart.**

Then open your arms.

**Wrap them around
the one you've chosen.
Hold them close.**

HUG!